by Carys S

Contents

© Carys Smith 2020.

Proofread: Eileen Harries
Editor: Jane Brookman
Special Advisors: Graham and Carol Whitaker
Publishing: Artbully, UK

Swimming against the Tide

We are the ones always too cold always.
Too far out; swimming against the tide of taboos.

We plunge right in up to our necks.
Drifting too far left or right; pulling
against the current of current opinion.

We never hang back or pause at the water's edge
for fear of swimming too fast or too far out.

We are the ones always in the cold, always.
Yet having heart enough to swim against the tide.

We are always, too cold, always. But not moaning
Stevie, nor drowning, just waving.

inspired by the poem Not waving but drowning: Stevie Smith 1957

Orange Juice:
1956

Kaz ran into the living room trailed by her younger sister. Dad was watching the horses on the black and white television Grandad Cyril had given them. The curtains were drawn so the picture would be clear. He was a dark heavy lump sprawled large across the settee.

“Dad! Dad!” said Kaz.

Kenneth shifted his gaze for a moment to look at this little interruption. “What?”

“We want to know something Dad.” Kaz carried on boldly; just out of reach to avoid the anticipated swipe that always came if he was disturbed watching his horses.

Carol Margaret, less cautious in nature and more indulged by their father, tugged at his sleeve:

“We want to know why those Don...Donal...Donaldsons and number...what number Kaz?”

“Get on with it kids or clear off back outside.” Kenneth waved his folded newspaper at them and kept his eyes firmly fixed on the finish line.

“It’s number twelve. Donaldson and number twelve,” Kaz said breathless, wanting desperately to know the answer but afraid of a slap. Dad’s hands were very big and very hard. “Why have they got orange juice along with their milk? Why has our orange juice stopped coming?”

Kenneth threw his paper down: three horses, two losers. There goes his three way bet. He struggled out of the sagging sofa and stomped to the window and pulled open the curtains. Across the waste ground he could just make out the two houses. The bottles of milk and orange juice were still waiting on the steps of seven and twelve. It was well into the afternoon. He thought about that for a moment. If they could leave milk and orange juice out that long they must have more than enough inside.

He shook out a cigarette and struck a match. “Have you heard of Robin Hood?” he said, blowing an impressive smoke ring into the air.

The two girls followed its path up to the ceiling, “More Dad! More Dad!” they both yelled, momentarily forgetting their quest.

Their father blew more rings and then a long stream of smoke from each nostril; tricks he had picked up from his time conscripted into the army. He could peel an apple or a potato, in one long strip. He could cut the skin of an orange into eight without hurting the fruit. He could play the spoons and the comb and paper. When he went to work at Woolwich Arsenal docks he carried a big hook in his belt. Sometimes he came home with a black eye and when asked “Who won Dad?” he would always say, “I didn’t come second.”

He was their Dad. They feared and revered him in equal measure. They shook their heads and waited.

“Robin Hood was a hero of the working classes like us.” He studied the deserted neighbourhood. Empty: the quiet time of a Saturday afternoon. "He robbed from the rich and shared it with the poor." He stubbed out his cigarette and made his way to the outside lav. newspaper tucked under his arm.

The girls followed him to the outhouse. He turned and gave them a quick sly grin. "Go careful and watch that old biddy's net curtains at five." He jerked open the door, adding as it closed behind him, "Robin kept some of the loot of course, for him and his merry men."

The two looked at each other doubtfully and hesitated in case Dad might offer any further advice. Kenneth dropped his trousers, opened his newspaper and called as an afterthought, "Charity begins at home remember. So bring us a bottle of milk."

*

The February afternoon was raw and bitter. Black ice slides had been on the pavements for weeks. They skirted carefully around them and made for the waste ground that divided the two sets of council houses. Carol Margaret wiped her constantly dripping nose on her sleeve. Kaz shoved bare chilblained hands into the pockets of her skimpy coat. They walked on in silence. Kaz thought about Robin Hood and imagined being a merry man. Carol Margaret kept an eye on the net curtains of number five. She was far more her father's daughter than Kaz would ever be.

The girls came at the houses from the corner end, hoping over the short dividing walls to number seven; then leapt the final two, each gripping a clinking bottle of orange juice. Carol Margaret, with a delicate hand, lifted the latch to the gate of number twelve and held it open whilst Kaz on silent terrified feet, flew to the step, grabbed the slippery milk bottle, knocking over the others as she fled. A net curtain fluttered, they heard a door begin to pull open, a shout, but they were gone, skidding and slipping, hanging onto their booty, running all the way to the Puffing Billy's abandoned outbuildings.

It was dark as they floundered their way home through the muddy snow-melt with the milk bottle cold and damp inside Kaz's coat. She wondered if David Donaldson would miss his orange juice and was sorry. His baby sister had the whooping cough. There was a nasty sourness at the back of her throat. It had not tasted as good as she had thought, either.

The boy girls

November 1962

Rob was a good six inches taller than Kaz. Kaz was slight, wiry, swift as a whippet. Rob was broad shouldered, stocky legged, a giant at fourteen. Kaz liked Rob because it was good to have a "bully buster." Rob liked Kaz because it was good to have a "homework cribber." They were best mates: inside and outside school.

Rob's house was full of hulking, fighting boys. Kaz's was full of screaming, fighting girls. They both preferred to be outside: in the woods where they smoked Kaz's Dad's Woodbines or in the park eating mini crunchies filched from Rob's family Christmas cupboard.

"Fancy Gravesend Park?" Rob said when they met on their corner. "I've money for the bus. We could go to that playground. Those two girls might turn up."

Kaz kicked at a stone sending it into the long grass and stuck chapped hands in pockets. "It's already cold and nearly dark."

"Dark is good isn't it? For the girls I mean."

Kaz thought about the cold then about the girls. Angie was a good kisser. It was a laugh under the bridge. No one knew them in Gravesend.

"Alright but can you nick Graham's hat for me again?"

"I can do better than that," said Rob pulling out a checked Andy cap from his pocket, "It was me Grandad's. I took it from the charity bag last night."

They saw the Number Eleven on the other side of the road. Kaz streaked across and swung on the pole one foot still on the pavement until Rob stumbled onto the platform just as the bell rang. Rob fished in his pocket for the coppers, grabbing the tickets as they came straight from the reel. They leapt the stairs two at a time away from the conductor's curses.

It was nearly five when they got to the park. There was a hint of fog. The gate was shut but they knew the way in through the broken fence behind the bushes. They walked in silence towards the playground keeping an eye out for the park keeper, then stood in the shelter of the bridge watching out for the twin shadows of the girls.

They came at last, their whispers overloud. Rob gave a whistle, Kaz, a passable attempt at an owl hoot. They met at the swings.

"Go on," said Angie, "Give us a swing."

The girls slid onto the swings, gripped the chains and waited. Rob and Kaz pinched their cigarette halves and stuck them behind an ear. They propelled the girls into the air until their arms ached and the girls' feet were level with the top bar. Their laughter echoed into the foggy night. They fell giddy into the waiting arms of Rob and Kaz.

"Coming to the bridge?" said Rob to the girl in the fur hooded anorak. The four stood in a semi circle breath steaming, feet stamping against the cold. The two girls exchanged a furtive look.

"I don't mind," said Angie taking Kaz's hand.

Rob put an arm round the girl and hurried her through the bridge to the far end. Kaz stopped just inside and felt against the dank stone wall finding somewhere dry for Angie to lean.

"You a right little gentleman aren't you?" Said Angie

"Not really." Kaz shrugged waiting, dry mouthed for her to start the kissing. Soon the giggles and play screams, the slapped hands from further up faded. Kaz gave in to the moment. It was scary but felt so good.

"Why do you two always wear caps?" Angie said, breaking the spell, "Are you bald already?"

Before Kaz could stop her she pulled off the cap, hands feeling for hair. Fingers found the rubber banded pony tail, brushed the metal hair clips either side.

"Oh...what are you?" she said with a slow laugh, "a gypsy boy or...a...girl?"

Kaz stepped back. They exchanged a hard stare. Kaz fought the urge to run.

"What if I was? Does it matter?"

Angie pressed her lips together and looked harder. She put out a hand and pulled Kaz back pressing their two bodies together until they fit.

“Not to me.” She said opening her coat, placing Kaz’s hands on small breasts, “but our brothers might not like it.”

*

They arranged to meet on the following Wednesday. They went in as before: through the broken fence behind the bushes, the stealthy walk towards the playground, waiting for the shelter of the bridge before they shared the cigarette and struck the match.

Kaz began to think about Angie and checked a pocket for the stolen lipstick from Woolworth’s. Would Angie put it on? She flexed numb fingers thinking of those soft breasts. Would it be ok to touch them under her jumper, like Rob did with Jill?

They heard footsteps on the gravel, soft voices behind them. A beam of light snapped on from the far end. It travelled to their feet and then up into their startled grey faces.

“That’s the little buggers.” said a deep guttural voice. “Mess with our sisters would you?”

Another torch snapped on. Three elongated shadows climbed the stone wall, outsized hands holding sticks. One drew back a catapult. A stone whizzed past their ears and pinged off the wall.

“Dirty Lezzers!”

Footsteps charged forward, a hail of sharp missiles ricocheting off stone before they even had time to think about running. One hit Kaz smack in the ear making her yelp.

Another caught Rob on the back of the head. Rob faltered pushing aside her cap feeling for blood.
Kaz grabbed Rob's elbow. "Run. Run!"

"That's it cry like the little girls you are!"

The big boys chased them right through the park. Kaz and Rob ran slipping through the duck pond uncaring of wet feet and towards the gap in the fence. It was blocked by milk crates. They turned this way and that in the cold dark, caught by an ambush of brambles.

For a moment Kaz gave up. Rob was too slow. They were going to get beaten; murdered even. Heavy feet were pushing through the undergrowth. There was a snap of elastic and a whiz of stones; shouts, filthy names, threats.

Far off they heard the rumble and a warning whistle. Kaz remembered the Puffing Billy line and the wooden slats across the rails if you were quick. Last summer they had played chicken and dare with the Goods train until they were caught. Kaz's Dad had laughed but Rob's had clouted both their ears.

They scrambled through the ditch and onto the cutting. The rails glinted silver in the half light from the signal box. They could see the rushing shape of the train. They could feel the vibrations as they hopped skipped and jumped their way over just in time.

They waited until the monster-train dashed by. Rob held a hand to the back of her head, blood squeezed through her fingers and down the back of her neck. Kaz stood legs and lips trembling watching in case their assailants decided to continue the chase, relief washing over as one called:

“Stay out of our park and away from our girls.”

The biggest one with the catapult sent a final sharp rocket across.”Next time we’ll get you and show you what a real man’s got between his legs.”

They went off laughing into the fog.

Rob and Kaz walked all the way home to Dartford. When they reached their corner Kaz said, “What’s a Lezzer?”

“Don’t know” said Rob. “Let’s go to Belvedere Park instead.”

Kaz shook her head, “I don’t know about that.” She took off the cap. “See you tomorrow at school.”

When she got in Dennis from next door was waiting in the kitchen. Her Mum had made him a cup of tea. He stood up red faced. She saw he was wearing the cream sweater she had said she liked, the one with Elvis stitched on the pocket.

“Dennis came round to see if you wanted to go to the pictures on Saturday Kaz.” Mum said her tone over bright.

She looked at Dennis and then at her Mum. Her ear smarted. She pushed the cap deeper into her pocket and gave Dennis her best smile.

“Alright then,” she said.

Beatie's Bomb

August 1941

(remembered by Beatrice Atkinson 1903-1987)

Everyone felt the blast before they heard it. Cyril was blown through the front door, his hand still clamped to his tin helmet, yelling a pointless warning. Betty, without thinking, thrust Teddy the Pekinese into the sideboard cupboard. Beatie had a fleeting thought to thank God that Sylvia Margaret was safe in Norfolk. Then walls folded inward, the roof crashed through ceilings, the floor crumpled sending them spiralling into the basement before the sound caught up: a whoosh, a terrifying screaming roar, bursting eardrums, stretching skin, a shredding of clothes.

The land mines had begun dropping just as the sun had dipped behind the skyline. Betty had wanted to go up to bed and take her chances but Beatie the eldest had the last word. They were preparing for another night in the Anderson, waiting for the kettle to boil to make up the flasks, searching for Teddy's basket, listening for Cyril so they could lock and board up the shop. Beatie had sensed the vibrations first, had felt the cold sweep of air, heard the shrieking before anyone else and knew this was *her* bomb, the one that would decide whether she was to live or die in this war.

The sacks of flour, sugar and sand saved them from instant death. Luck prevented them being crushed by falling furniture and debris but the choking dust had them gasping. Beatie tore at the remains of her apron throwing it across her face. She lay prone, heart thumping, throat constricting, eyes wide open trying to see through cloth and grey fug. She thought she could see searchlights probing the sky; the red glow of firestorm. The drone of planes was still overhead; a thousand angry buzzing bees in a blind fury. The emergency sirens were at full blast, the anti-aircraft guns pop-popping somewhere south of the river The bombs still fell, sharp and near, muffled and far. She listened for Cyril, for Betty, thought she heard Teddy whimpering somewhere behind her. There was something else. She strained to hear. Her blood ran cold as she recognised the steady hum of the gas fridge. She half smiled. Cyril had told her ***GEC*** were reliable but did they have to be *this* reliable? Beatie hoped she'd had her bomb, that there wasn't another explosion to come. And then, quite suddenly, she fell asleep and dreamed of green parks, wide rivers and bird song.

*

That was one of the longest nights of the war. Beatie had drifted in and out of sleep for the best part of a night and day, another night and then half of another day. She awoke to a swollen tongue, cracked lips and a dreadful thirst. The fridge was still murmuring its presence. She pictured the ice lollies she had made from squash in the freezer, wondered if anything was left of the milk, realised that the wet in her mouth was the iron taste of blood. She probed for the missing tooth. At least it was at the back. She tried to call out. Nothing came but a strangled croak. She shifted a hand, grabbed brick dust and threw it. She listened hard. There was that eerie silence of aftermath when survivors crept through the ruined streets and picked through their belongings in whispers.

Beatie grabbed more brick dust and threw to where she was sure there were the faint sounds of voices, a lifting and a shifting of wood, feet not far away, a clink of shovels; Teddy whining somewhere. Carefully she peeled away the cloth from her eyes. An orange mote of light cut dimly through the dust. Beatie threw more silt. They were digging a tunnel. They were coming. She drifted off again. This time she dreamed of cool jugs of water, dripping taps and a yapping sound of dog.

The shaft of light was longer now, the muted voices clearer. She could see shoes and legs above the diminishing brick mountain. Caught a voice she may have recognised. Mrs Lambert? Fanny Cartwright? Then a clear exchange:

"Look at all this butter and tea Fan."

"We can't take it." Yes that was Fanny Cartwright. "We can't steal from Cyril and Beatie."

"They took a direct hit Fan. That's why they've left this one til last. When they do dig it will only be for bodies...here quick we can share what's left."

"Well alright then. I suppose we won't be the only ones taking from the dead to feed the living."

"Cyril loved his Old Holborn," said a male voice. Arthur Hadley?

"Well, it's no good to him now is it?" that was Eric Ward. She was sure of it.

Beatie pictured their stock buried in the rubble. She could hear feet and hands sifting through the bricks and mortar of their home. She was helpless, legs trapped and bleeding; the still working fridge a constant threat, her voice silenced. She had no idea why she began to think of Dickens and Scrooge. He was robbed of his dignity in death too. But he deserved it, didn't he? They weren't dead. They were waiting for a rescue whilst her neighbours scrambled to get at tins and tea, butter, sugar, flour and their children quarrelled over broken sweet jars.

From somewhere close by she heard Cyril begin to cough and Betty begin sobbing. She grappled for more than dust, found a small sharp object and half rose to throw it as hard and as far as she could. It fell limply short of the opening but miraculously her voice returned and she called and called and called. Teddy began barking wildly, scrabbling at the cupboard he was trapped in.

Other familiar voices of customers and neighbours filtered through the opening, saying they were coming, shouting threats after those shuffling away with their loot. Quickly the tunnel widened and snaked towards them. The fridge abruptly cut off and a tall shadow knelt beside her, a sandy coloured little Peke under one arm.

"You've had your bomb Beatie love," said Cyril, wiping a cut across his eye on a filthy ragged sleeve.

Her bomb, "Beatie's bomb," as it became known in the family had fallen on her just as she had predicted, yet they were all alive, even precious little Teddy. Things were only things. Those looters were just desperate people in a war torn city. But family, her still living breathing family, was everything.

The private war of Private Cyril Atkinson

(1902-1988)
April 15th 1945

I was part of the Infantry marching behind the heavy armour. I always kept close to my favourite anti-tank gun because you never knew when...They used to call me "Dead-eye Dick." I got a Marksman medal. I'd had plenty of practice before I went to war on the Ack Ack guns...anti aircraft guns. When I was made Corporal I used to lead the march...then they called me The Merry Whistler. I reckon I was made Corporal just because of my whistling...funny that because I can't sing for toffee. They called me Uncle when I was in charge of the mobile kitchen unit...I'll make you my curried beans if you like. No?

Your Grandma and your Auntie Betty went to Europe in the '60's on a holiday. They went to France, Belgium and Holland. I stayed home. I told her "I've walked every square mile of those places already Beatie." When I went on holiday I liked to forget not remember. See this silver cigarette case? This was your Great Grandad's. He used to keep it inside his uniform, over his heart, during the first War. He told me to do the same. See this dent...I nearly copped it that time...and this one nearly got Father. He gave it me when I was sent to France.

It took almost a year to walk from France to Germany. We walked in all seasons and had some nasty scraps on the way. Antwerp was the worst. I was getting on by then...war is a young man's game...but they needed all the cannon fodder they could get if we were going to beat Mr Hitler. When the shop got blown I lost my reserved occupation...and ended up a soldier. All that walking...all that war...all that...never mind...I better get back in the garden it looks like rain...

*

Cyril never minded sharing that part of his war. It served as an explanation as to why he was such a good walker, even into his eighties and why he never left "Old Blighty" once he came home. But if you asked him about the part his regiment had played in liberating Bergen-Belsen his whole face would close down. His hands would fumble for his tobacco tin and busy themselves rolling wafer thin cigarettes until it was full. Then he would look out the kitchen window, put down his tea cup and say: "Looks like rain Petsy. I better get back out and finish the lawn."

Bergen-Belsen April 15th 1945

In the early morning, once the heavy armour had gone on ahead, their noise and smell fading, Cyril and his unit began to file through the narrow country lanes before crossing into the orchards. Confronted with an unexpected near silence and the sweet fragrance of fruit blossom his whistling faltered. Only the tramp of feet and the lumbering rattle of light artillery on mud hardened tracks rivalled the dawn chorus. He counted the different fruits promised by the pink and white blossom. He wondered how their trees at home were doing. Was their allotment still standing on the outskirts of Hackney Downs? How was father managing? Had Beatie found them a home?

In the distance they saw a farmhouse freshly whitewashed. No smoke came from the chimney nor was a soul to be seen. Yet the pastures were littered with tranquil cattle, sheep and a few plough horses. It was the same as they passed through the small town. Just quiet rows of blank-eyed windows as if its occupants had silently stolen away during the night.

Within minutes of leaving the outskirts they had reached the barbed wire surrounding the camp. The smell and the stench came first, obliterating all memory of the sweet smell of orchard-scent and rich green fields. Cyril pulled up sharply just before the gate, the footfall behind him slowly grinding to a halt. He felt himself sway, the air leave his lungs. They were so near the pleasant farmhouse and the seemingly innocent town, yet nothing but filth, pestilence and death were in all four corners. The ragged occupants, more skeleton than skin, listless and covered in lice wandered past. They lurched on rickety legs, sightlessly stepping over bodies, too starved and sick to celebrate their freedom.

"Corporal Atkinson, quick march man!" the Sergeant Major's bellow barely penetrated his racing heart and mind. Cyril hesitated, dragged a leg forward and then the other. There were mutters and retching from the line. He knew with horrible certainty that they were about to witness sights even more unspeakable and incomprehensible. He shook himself, stood tall, yelled a "forward...MARCH" and began to whistle "The White Cliffs of Dover."

The silence of this place
Where no birds sing,
This pit of hell, where trees enshroud
As walls, to hide the shame.

The earth is wet with tears,
Making dark rivers in these paths of mud
There stands their shrine, these nameless ones
A lonely finger pointing to the sky
The conscience of the world in sallow stone,
The sorrow of the world, written in blood.

(Anthony Rawlings 7th Armoured Division 1951)

(This fragment was found folded and tucked into the sheath holding the Campaign Medals awarded to Cyril Morris Atkinson...my Grandfather was not a reading man...not even a newspaper)

10 weeks

Pontypridd 16 August 2020
Extract from the diary of an Outlander

It's been ten weeks. I still feel like a time traveller. My step is just as cautious. There are fewer shuttered shops but the same respectful queues. There are more masks, more people but fewer policemen and women to guard our calm and quelled streets. The homeless must be continuing to be homed...somewhere (?) What a compliant race we have become. The fear of CORONA has crushed the fire of rebellion in all our bellies it seems.

My careful feet tread the two meter circles to Prince's. It's closed but activity is going on inside. There are no signature currant buns or meringues on the shelves; no bread, large or small, white or brown to be seen. I turn and climb the steps to the Indoor Market which has a hand scrawled sign on its step bravely stating ***"We are open for business...if not as usual!"***

The Fountain Cafe with cleaner-than- before plastic flowered table cloths is open. There is hand gel on the counter but no sticky sauce bottles on the tables. Twelve thirty and not packed to the gunnels? Gracie had left the kitchen to chat to the woman who cleans the toilets. Yes there is more than "just one open public toilet" now but they don't look that COVID clean to me.

I order tea and toast when she comes back and wait for less than five minutes. For once the radio music is not a garbled tinny background but rather like a full orchestra bouncing off the four corners of the almost empty room; Gene Pitney and his pitiless and crass "24 hours from Tulsa." It sounds somehow more repellent at full blast.

Old Alice comes in muttering about "blasted masks steaming up me glasses" then "no circular buses" and of course "my old legs." She orders the full English and says:

"Well Gracie don't anyone know you're open? How many have you had in today?"

Gracie reads straight from her order pad in a resigned monotone:

Your full English
Five coffees
Two tea and toasts

Immediately I feel guilty. Surely I could have eaten the full English or ordered a piece of plastic wrapped Swiss roll? I feel worse when the cost is only "£1.65 love" as Boris is picking up the fifty percent. I leave hating to have to thank Boris for anything.

The Fountain is the only cafe open in this Covid-19 new-world Indoor Market. There is no "business as usual" anywhere in our flood-wracked then plague-wracked valleys town.

I walk back to the Car Park which is still free just in case we might have to come here.

The A470 is busier. There are still plenty of the yellow and blue blaring emergencies. I comfort myself with the thought that now days they are probably not all about the virus:

some more palatable personal tragedy; stroke, heart attack, accident, perhaps.

As I park the car and turn the key to my safe house I think:

“In ten more weeks maybe this will all start to fade into the history books.” But then another torrential raincloud blots out the hopeful August sunshine.

I amend that thought: “Or ten weeks after the next ten weeks...maybe.”

To Post or Not to Post...that is the Question
Extract from the diary of an Outlander
Church Village 7th September 2020

Even the simplest everyday things have changed since COVID. How different could posting a parcel be, I asked myself. Yet still, I felt apprehensive as soon as I saw the dour faced man behind the gigantic Perspex screen. For a start he flinched as I took my place on the blue circle marked ***2mt.*** He flinched again as I stretched my arms forward to place the parcel on the scales. He flinched so hard I thought he might topple off his chair.

He frowned: "That's going to be expensive, that is," he said. "Are you sure you want to post it?"

I had been sure. Very sure but...

"Have you got one of these?" he ripped off a small label, "Customs. If you don't fill this in they'll just chuck it away...COVID...have you got your own pen? With COVID it's better if you've got your own pen."

I scrabbled around my bag and pulled out a leaky biro. With a finger tip he pushed the label under the screen. I completed it and then stuck it on the parcel.

"New Zealand?" he said, "Are you sure you want to post it there? Auckland is shut for freight. They've a second wave of COVID. Your parcel might never arrive...or months from now." He gave me a searching look and repeated "COVID."

I was sure. I had been very sure but...

“Shall I let the next one in and give you some thinking time?” he said, his tone hopeful.

I shook my head and took it to the big packet and parcels window. He shrugged; checked the label, examined the Sellotape and the return address from a distance with troubled eyes.

“£23.46...air mail. Still you’re better off with air mail. It might just arrive...COVID.”

The next customer was pacing outside looking well and truly pissed off in the drizzle. I pulled out my purse to pay.

“Can you pay by card because...”

“I know,” I cut in, “COVID.” I produced my card.

“Keep the receipt...just in case,” he said then added, “People are very worried you know. They’re scared to come in.”

“What? Scared to come in here? Scared of what?” but I already knew the answer...COVID.

“All this paper: envelopes, parcels, letters, postcards.” He counted them off on his fingers, as if they were somehow the world’s COVID culprits.

“But the science doesn’t support that.” I said taking a step back. “There’s no evidence that COVID lives on those things for more than a millisecond.”

He shook his head so hard I thought it might drop off or at least snap at the neck. “Maybe not but...who knows what COVID can or can’t do?”

For a long moment we regarded each other through the partition. Was there some private COVID 19 sorrow behind his gloomy prognosis? I felt sad as I imagined a lost friend or family member, then guilty. Had I put this trusty, if humourless public servant at risk? The science, as they keep telling us, is not exact and can change. Was there something still waiting to be understood about stationery?

I remembered the constant blaring of the blue and yellow just a few months back. I thought about how they were making a new sinister reappearance this past week: the local lockdowns, the masks, the visors, the empty buses.

“You’re alright though, aren’t you?” I rallied. “Do you know anyone who’s got it from paper products?”

“No but it doesn’t mean someone hasn’t...you can’t trust this COVID, not with the post or anything.”

The man outside began to tap on the window with his bundle of envelopes. The drizzle was now rain. He reluctantly put my parcel in the half full grey jute bag behind him. I began to edge towards the door. As I made my side stepping escape in the doorway I heard him greet his next customer with:

“Are you sure you want to send all those?”

“Don’t let the old man In”

Rosie Brown:

Rosie Browne was already in her night clothes and slippers when the knock came. She pressed pause on the remote and went grumbling under her breath to the front door. Why was Arthur so early? Where was his key?

Through the glass there were two dark uniformed shadows. Her step faltered, she muttered, “What the...” then hurried to unlock the door.

“I don’t understand,” she said again, “What do you mean my Arthur’s been found dead? Where? How? Why?” Her hand groped for her inhaler and twisted, she took a quick breath and then thrust it aside. She searched her dressing gown pocket for the pack of Silver Cut and box of matches she always kept for emergencies.

“Shall I make us a cup of tea?” said the young female officer, glancing from her Sergeant and then at Rosie.

At his nod she went off, relieved, into the kitchen. She took her time arranging the cups and saucers, finding the tea and milk, filling the kettle. Her first murder and it would have to be someone she knew. Why would anyone want to kill Arthur like that; shot in the knees and the head gang-land style? He was just the local plumber. Everyone liked Arthur.

“They did it,” Rosie took a swallow of tea and lit a new cigarette from the smouldering fag-end. “It’s them that’s been breaking in up and down these streets.” She paused allowing the deep cough to rattle round her chest. "It's them that took nearly all Arthur's tools from his van."

Sergeant Blake put down his tea cup and stood. "You should have someone stay with you tonight Rosie. Is your Derek still living nearby?"

She ignored his suggestion. Instead she stubbed out her smoke and leant across the table.

"You know it's them Ted." Her flint grey eyes stared into his. "Bring them in before they scarper. They're already on bail and it was Arthur's statement that got them there."

"We've got more than one line of enquiry already," he said, dropping his eyes, folding his notebook into his top pocket. "We *will* get who's done this, you can be sure of that."

"Can I?" said Rosie, picking up the tea tray and turning her back. "You two see yourselves out. Don't worry, I'll phone Derek in a minute, I don't want any of those Victim Support visits neither."

*

Rosie waited six weeks before deciding to sort through Arthur's work shed. She waited in case there was an arrest or if those "developments" Ted Blake promised came to anything. She waited until she heard that they had all got "cast iron alibis. Of course they had. Once Derek started on about cleaning out the shed himself she knew it was time to get on with the job.

She dressed in Arthur's old boiler suit, his navy Smith's beanie and his Wellington boots. He might not be here in the flesh but now at least he was in spirit. In the front pocket of the suit she had a quart bottle of Jameson's whiskey. Under her arm she carried their old CD player with a disc slotted in ready.

The shed was just as he had left it; neat and well swept; everything had a place and was in its place. Luckily those scum bags hadn't known about the shed half hidden as it was behind the old oaks at the far end of their garden. Rosie leant against the work bench. Whenever she thought of those bastards she had a serious rush of blood to the head. Her heart began to beat a tattoo, her hands clenched into fists. They had kicked Ernie Saunders half to death last week when he had found them in his garage. He had more or less admitted it was them but, like the rest, he was too afraid to go to the Police. What would they do anyway? Only her Arthur had that kind of nerve and where had that got him? Still, she wouldn't have had him any other way.

"To you Arthur love." She said lifting the whiskey bottle to her lips and taking a long swig. "I won't let you down."

She clicked on the CD and hummed along to "Don't let the old man in." Arthur had always said that Toby Keith must have written that song as much for him as for Clint Eastwood. He was right: he had never let the old man in and nor would she.

She kept one steadying hand on the bench and did a slow mental inventory, starting from the near corner with its tools hung according to height and weight; then along the centre panel at the boxes of spare parts before she found what she was looking for; the six kilo bottle of propane gas already fitted with the necessary piping fixed onto his heavy duty wheeler. The tins of oil paint and the bottle of white spirit were in the far corner. All she needed to do was to fit the canvas bag from her shopping trolley over the lot and it was good to go.

Later she emptied the rest of the whiskey into her cup of Horlicks and left it cooling whilst she texted the Vicar:

> ***"I can call the Bingo this Friday. Feeling up to it. Doing what Arthur would have wanted."***

*

On Friday nights the gang met in the derelict building by the old Puffing Billy line. The entire neighbourhood knew what they were doing there: divvying up, counting the cash, bagging heroin, snorting coke, and smoking their weed. Everyone kept well away, including the Police, it seemed. On a Monday to Friday early evening though, it was just a bit of waste ground that people took shortcuts through. Rosie always took the shortcut to the Church Hall on a Friday to call the bingo. She had being doing it for years and no one took any notice. Sometimes her Arthur had walked across with her to the Late-Stop betting shop. Now she made a lonely figure but she did the journey every week just the same. She wasn't about to "Let the old man in."

Two weeks before he had been murdered she and Arthur had looked over the building carefully; found the broken breeze blocks; broken a few more and then replaced them. On the way home they had discussed their plan. As always he had been right. It *was* easy. She slipped on a pair of yellow Marigolds, fresh from the packet and took out the blocks. Arthur had made the hole just big enough for the gas cylinder to slide in. Her arm followed, threading the pipe through the gap they had made. Then she prised open the oil paints and upended the white spirit. Finally she switched the valve to ON, waited a second for the pleasing sound of escaping gas before quickly and carefully replacing each block. It would only take a few minutes to reach the Church Hall. There would be just enough time to help sell the bingo cards and get the number bag ready. She walked with a light step pulling the empty shopping trolley behind her marvelling at how perfect the weather was behaving: ideally humid with not even a sniff of a wind.

*

Rosie drew out another disc and waved it in the air deliberately tantalising her audience. They waited with baited breath, licking the stubs of their pencils, adjusting their glasses, looking over the shoulders of those in front trying to see how many unmarked squares they had left.

“Twenty four knock on the door...twenty...four. Two four...24.” Rosie gave a quick glance at the lopsided clock on the wall opposite: seven thirty already.

“Thirty nine make them mine” she improvised, “Three and nine...39.”

The crowd gave a collective groan. This was the full house game with the cash prize.

“Thirteen. Unlucky for some,” Rosie called, as the clock hand ticked forward another minute. “One and three...13.”

She shook the discs and paused.

“Get on wiv it Rosie,” Sheila yelled from the back, fanning her flushed face with her paper.

A sudden white light lit up the dingy room. No one looked behind them. Each pair of eyes was fixated on their numbers. All ears were tuned to Rosie’s next call. Someone had to be the Winner.

“Sixty two...”Rosie grinned into the bag, “Six and two...tickity blew...62.”

The massive explosion flung the door off its hinges, the floorboards shifted and the windows rattled.

“Five. No man alive,” Rosie yelled triumphantly. “Five no man alive...5.”

“Bingo!” screamed Sheila running up the aisle flourishing her paper. “Full house!”

Everyone clapped.

Only on a Thursday
(part one)

Terri with a Y

Sally marvelled at the meticulous straight lines Terry always produced with the lawn mower. It was a picture; as lush and as flat as a bowling green. From the French doors she watched as he began to clip the edges along their new herbaceous border. He had such an eye. He could compete with Laurence Llewelyn Bowen for texture, taste and colour any day of the week.

She called a reminder that she was out for the whole afternoon; bridge then tea with Cousin Juliet. Terry looked up, smiled, waved and blew her a kiss, said:

"Take as long as you like dear. I've plenty to keep me going."

Sally sat to put on the new red sling back Dolce and Gabbana stilettos she had bought from Hewi's. Terry said they were scarlet not just plain old red. He was probably right. She turned her ankles, pointed her toes; they were gorgeous. They had cost a bomb but as Terry always said, "If you buy cheap you'll look cheap."

She picked up her bag and went into the hall, loving the crisp clack of heels on marble tile. What a wonderful indulgence to wear such high shoes. It was always low heels or sandals when she and Terry went out together. She towered above him even barefoot. *Only on a Thursday* could she wear the shoes she liked best. And bless him, Terry encouraged her every step of the way.

Terry put his tools into the wheelbarrow, emptied the grass onto the compost and carefully tidied the lawn mower back into the shed. With an unhurried tread he went into the house and up the three flights until he stood under the attic. The hook was where they always left it, in the corner by the spare bathroom. It was just long enough for him to catch hold of the eye to pull down the step ladder. He paused, patted his pocket, felt the reassuring outline of the key and climbed the steps carefully.

His hand fumbled for the double switch. Light flooded the room transforming it into a brilliant stage set. Soft soundproofed cork covered the floor, pale mint plaster board the walls and rafters. A huge wardrobe stood on the right of the window; a porcelain sink unit with a square mirror to the left. A selection of expensive creams; a travel Lady-shave kit and a makeup bag well stocked with assorted lipsticks and mascara were evenly spaced on the shelf beneath.

Terry went to the wardrobe and unlocked the door letting it swing open. On the inside was a long oblong piece of glass, behind him an old fashioned dresser's mirror. He stood for a moment, smiling at his double reflection, raised an eyebrow before striking a vaudeville pose:

"Time to go Terry," he said.

Terri crossed the lawn, keeping to the evenly spaced stepping stones, loving the crisp clack of heels on paving. She was pleased with the dandelion yellow print dress from John Lewis; it was just the right colour; bright and energetic for a breezy Spring day like this. The tan suede heels were an excellent match. With a kid gloved hand she swung the clematis covered panel to one side revealing a back gate. From an elegant leopard print mini Windsor handbag, a particular favourite of hers, she drew out another brass key and paused for a quick glance into her vanity mirror.

"Hello Terri," she said, smiling a welcome at her reflection. She took a deep breath, gave her lips a final coating of WOW and settled the pixie cut, human hair wig one last time. Then she straightened her shoulders, lifted her head, unlocked the gate and went out into her brave new world.

It was just a short walk to Penarth cliff tops. Terri smiled a good afternoon at the old gentleman who raised his hat. She exchanged a knowing smile with the young mother labouring a pram up the slight incline. Cioni's Bistro was just ahead. Her tea date was already waiting just inside the covered doorway.

"Oh there you are," said Cousin Juliet, "Right on time as usual. Shall we go in?"

The two air-kissed and smiled their thanks to the admiring grey-haired man who stepped aside holding the door. Their usual Thursday afternoon table, overlooking the public golf course and the sea was ready. There was the small bouquet of cornflowers and pink carnations in the cut glass vase, the sandwich and cake stand, the flower cushioned seats, the ornamental candle, everything as it always was. O*nly on a Thursday*.

"I just love those gorgeous shoes Juliet," said Terri, "They're not just plain old red though, are they? I'd call them scarlet. Let me guess, Dolce and Gabanna?"

Only on a Thursday
(part two)

TerrY with an i

What would I like to talk about? My other life I suppose, when I'm the other Terri.
***S*.......**

Yes you can call me Terry, Samantha...Terry with an i.
***S*.......**

No dear. You're asking the wrong question. It should be "When did I start dressing as ***me***...the other ***me***. Better still ask: when did I identify my heart's life.
***S*.......**

Yes...my ***heart's*** life.
***S*.......**

I will if you're sure you're interested.
***S*.......**

Thank you then. I was a late bloomer, you might say. I was already 38 or 39. It must have been 1972, perhaps 73. The wife and I both had parts in the local Am-Dram she was the Geni I was cast as Widow Twanky...yes Aladdin... she was the Geni. Anyway I was reluctant at first. I took plenty of persuading I can tell you.

But from the moment that wig went on...oh...not just the wig but the whole ensemble... silk stockings, the push up bra padded with silicone, the pan makeup, mascara, lipstick...I felt...and it's still the same today... I felt transformed into the real ***me***...my ***heart's*** me.

S...........

No, it's not a problem for me. I really am *not* Gay. Trans then? Not likely!

No of course I don't think I'm living a lie. I like being Terry with a y. Terry the husband; Terry the father, Terry the mate down the pub, Grampy Terry, especially Grampy Terry. Oh and Terry in the garden and Terry with his man shed. All of *that is* me...the *other* me.
S.........

What troubles me then? It's just so stressful to be a man all the time ...tiring...all those straight lines along the grass; all that DIY; the high powered job; the endless talk about football or worse, cricket. There are plenty of men like me I can assure you.
S.......

I'm glad you see what I mean.

S.......

Do I think there should be secrets between husband and wife? No dear, I don't...but a prevarication perhaps; an unspoken acknowledgement maybe; a knowing we're both in this together...

Elf's 400th night.

Elf woke with a start. It was four twenty *again.* Every night it was the same: two twenty then four twenty then seven fifteen. Elf shuffled to the bathroom and squeezed what was left from a bladder already wrung dry. Habit...if you wake it's got to be urine related; the older you get the more shrunken the bladder; or so it's said.

The cat stretched from the staircase and came to wind itself around the half bare elfin leg putting one delicate talon through the cotton pyjamas. This was now Kitty's routine too: food at two twenty, four twenty then seven fifteen. Elf stumbled down the stairs, eyes open only a crack, squinting in the half light or the half dark; features all uncannily elf-like.

Once back in bed Elf pulled the fleece over sensitive hands, another only at night phenomenon and tried to locate the reoccurring dream: the bland-faced Face Book chicken tried and then sentenced to the chopping block for the crime of Silence. This was inevitably followed by a walking towards the sea but never quite reaching it, or a perpetual swimming against the tide, until finally, not coming up for air; not waving but drowning.

Elf opened the iPad pressed onto Youtube in search of the ideal ***ten hours of soft, quiet relaxing music***. It was worth a try. It sometimes worked but not tonight. Tonight they were all harsh and jarring and loud- loud- loud. They were enough to cause elfsomnia. Elf clicked off iPad and turned to iPhone. **Watch** had plenty of ***Trump Bashing*** and for a while they amused and then angered and then bored Elf into complete wakefulness.

Elf hated to give in to the yell of the frustrated insomniac but yelled anyway, secure in the knowledge that the Old Witch next door was deaf and slept in the front bedroom. Elf wished elves still had tears but they had dried up months ago. Elf thought about a cup of Roobush tea but was afraid of heartburn. At night Elf was afraid of many things.

Elf turned literary and thought of all the poems written about Insomnia. Elf began to intone from memory ***"By the universe deserted,"*** Elizabeth Bishop, then Dana Giora's ***"The talking house."*** Elf listened hard but *this* house refused to talk. There was never a crack or a creak not even a windy rattle of a window pane; just the clanging bell of silence.

Eventually Elf gave up looking for Rossetti's ***"shred of sleep"*** and for a while allowed fevered images to flit in and out of a tired mind even though they were obviously ***"useless insights...a terrible clarity,"*** (Giora again) and all that.

Instead of sheep Elf began a count of famous people afflicted with the same malaise as humble Elf***: Vincent Van Gogh, painter, (***the ear***), Abraham Lincoln, president,*** (assassinated***), Marilyn Monroe, actress,*** *(suicide?)* ***Judy Garland, movie star*** *(bitch mother?)* ***Groucho Marx, comic actor*** *(surely not?)* Those names and those lives lived *did not* bode well for any insomniac to contemplate – that way indeed ***"madness lies."*** (King Lear)

There *was* music. Elf often took refuge in song even though a certain Pixie had said: "You do know you can't sing, don't you?" Regardless Elf sang a line or two from James Blunt: "***Once again I cannot sleep. I walk out the door and up the street. I look at the stars beneath my feet.***" From James Elf moved onto Passenger: "***the nights go on and on***" and then the whole ***Patchwork"*** album before returning to ***Watch*** and then back again to ***Youtube***. There had to be *one* ***stress relieving fall asleep fast to soft piano and sounds of nature,*** *somewhere* in their endless listings.

Daylight came creeping through the edges of the blackout blind and the thin cotton curtains. Elf lay in twisted sheets resigned and resentfully aware that it would soon be time to shed all nightly elfness; to crawl bleakly from an unslept bed back into the human form of the ever sleep-deprived Kaz. Vaguely, on the edge of something like sleep, Elf reached out once more for that nebulous dream- reason for the Face Book chicken and the significance of the disappearing sea. It was like a lantern burning somewhere near yet too far; or a distant lighthouse. Feeling full of cliché and exhaustion Elf wondered if tonight was the night when Elf/Kaz would grasp the nettle of excoriating honesty. Hay presto, abracadabra, cause and effect duly noted: goodbye insomnia.

Elf muttered: ***"O what ails thee Knight at Arms, alone and palely loitering?" (***John Keats.) But Elf fell sudden asleep and the second tranche of dreams chased through in rapid succession: lost hotel rooms, missing cars, broken down motorbikes and always, Elf endlessly chasing after setting suns all the while conscious of the sea, the sea, the sea, receding into the distance.

Thus ended Elfs 400th night.

The L Word

LGBTQI+

Her mouth opened *just* that "bliss of a kiss much" before she sat back. Hand to heart. Shock and regret floating across her face.

"I'm not ***L***esbian." She said.

And so I stepped away, pulled my chair knee touching close and said:

"Nor I. It's such an ugly word." Her hand rested heavy in my palm.

"I'm not ***G***ay then." She said leaving her knees and hand where they were.

"Nor I. It's an impossible word." I kissed her fingers. She let my lips linger before gently taking them under the table and onto her lap.

"Impossible?"

"Impossible. Who can be *that* happy all of the time?"

She gave a ghost of a smile. "I can't be **B**i. Not now at my age."

"No?" I placed a careful hand on her cheek, looked deep into those beautiful golden eyes. "But aren't you just a tiny bit ***b***i-curious?"

She flushed. Laughed a little, said, "A denial wouldn't be quite fair."

"Obviously you're not the ***T*** word. Transsexual." I paused, teetering on a knife edge. "Could you perhaps be... ***Q***?"

"**Q**ueer? Now *that's* an ugly word!"

Not **Q**ueer but...**Q**uestioning?"

"***I***?" She said slowly "***I*** don't know. Could ***I***? ***I*** could be. ***I*** suppose."

This time as I went in for the kiss of bliss there was no hand to heart, no shock or regret.

Later...much **l**ater I said, "**+** there is another L word."

"Another *L* word?" she turned to me, lifting her head from the pillow, "An L word you *will* accept?"

I nodded. "Oh yes definitely a much better L word."

"A better ***L*** word?" she said. Her smile was wide and knowing. How could she doubt me now?

I kissed the remains of pink from her lips and said

"Love is just love. That's my L word and I...Love you!"

Gin and Ego

Haiku to a straight lady (verb: to flirt)

An amorous act
A careless trifling with a heart
More tender than yours